Dear Parent:

Congratulations! Your child is taking the first steps on an exciting journey. The destination? Independent reading!

STEP INTO READING® will help your child get there. The program offers five steps to reading success. Each step includes fun stories and colorful art. There are also Step into Reading Sticker Books, Step into Reading Math Readers, Step into Reading Phonics Readers, Step into Reading Write-In Readers, and Step into Reading Phonics Boxed Sets—a complete literacy program with something to interest every child.

Learning to Read, Step by Step!

STEP 1 — Ready to Read **Preschool–Kindergarten**
• big type and easy words • rhyme and rhythm • picture clues
For children who know the alphabet and are eager to begin reading.

STEP 2 — Reading with Help **Preschool–Grade 1**
• basic vocabulary • short sentences • simple stories
For children who recognize familiar words and sound out new words with help.

STEP 3 — Reading on Your Own **Grades 1–3**
• engaging characters • easy-to-follow plots • popular topics
For children who are ready to read on their own.

STEP 4 — Reading Paragraphs **Grades 2–3**
• challenging vocabulary • short paragraphs • exciting stories
For newly independent readers who read simple sentences with confidence.

STEP 5 — Ready for Chapters **Grades 2–4**
• chapters • longer paragraphs • full-color art
For children who want to take the plunge into chapter books but still like colorful pictures.

STEP INTO READING® is designed to give every child a successful reading experience. The grade levels are only guides. Children can progress through the steps at their own speed, developing confidence in their reading, no matter what their grade.

Remember, a lifetime love of reading starts with a single step!

For my brave little girls,
Lilly and Lucy
—M.L.

 Published in the United States by Random House Children's Books, a division of Random House, Inc., 1745 Broadway, New York, NY 10019, and in Canada by Random House of Canada Limited, Toronto, in conjunction with Disney Enterprises, Inc.

ISBN: 978-0-7364-2916-0 (trade) — ISBN: 978-0-7364-8109-0 (lib. bdg.)

Printed in the United States of America 10

STEP INTO READING®

STEP 2

Disney · PIXAR

BRAVE

A Mother's Love

By Melissa Lagonegro

Illustrated by Maria Elena Naggi
and Studio IBOIX

Random House New York

Princess Merida is late.
The royal family waits.

Merida's mother
is the queen.

The queen teaches Merida
how to be a princess.
She shows Merida
how to play the harp.
Merida is bored.

Merida wants
to play with her sword.

The queen tells Merida
she must marry
the son of a lord.

It is her job

as the princess.

Merida is mad!

Merida gets ready
to meet some lords' sons.
She wears a fancy gown.
The queen is proud.

Merida is sad.
She does not want
to get married.

The young lords
will shoot arrows
at a target.

The best shooter
will marry the princess.

Merida joins the game.

She is the best.

She wins!

Now no one

can marry Merida.

The queen is mad.

The queen wants Merida
to get married.
Merida says no.

She cuts
the family tapestry.

Merida runs away.
She meets a Witch.
She asks the Witch
to change the queen.

The Witch makes a cake
that holds a spell.
The spell
will change the queen.

Merida returns
to the castle.
The queen eats
the spell cake.

The cake

changes the queen—

into a bear!

Merida did not want this.

Merida and her mother
look for the Witch.
They need her
to break the spell.
But the Witch is gone!

Merida and her mother
go fishing.
They have fun.

Merida and her mother
meet a mean bear.
They run back
to the castle.

Merida wants
to help her mother.
She wants to mend
the family tapestry.

Merida tells the lords
she will marry
one of their sons.
The queen stops her.
She wants Merida
to be happy.

The men chase the queen from the castle.

The queen is in trouble.
No one knows
she is the bear!
Merida protects her.

The mean bear returns!

The queen

protects Merida.

The two bears fight.

Merida fixes
the torn tapestry.
She and her mother hug.
The tapestry covers them.

The queen is
human again!
Love has
broken the spell.

Merida and the queen will always be mother and daughter. Now they are friends, too.